This Topsy and Tim book belongs to

_____

Topsy and Tim Go Green

By Jean and Gareth Adamson

One Friday afternoon Topsy and Tim came home from
school looking rather glum.
"Is something wrong?" said Dad.

"Miss Terry says the world is all messed up with rubbish and fumes and stuff," said Tim. "And there are so many people that there's no room left for wild animals," said Topsy.

"We could do something about it," said Mummy.
"We could recycle our rubbish, instead of throwing it away. That would help the poor old world."
Topsy and Tim cheered up and enjoyed their tea.

Next morning, after breakfast, Topsy and Tim helped
Dad to put lots of old bottles, piles of plastic cartons
and loads of old newspapers into boxes and bags.

Mummy and Dad packed everything into the car and they all drove off to the recycling centre. The bottles clinked and chinked all the way.

The recycling bins stood in the supermarket car park.
Dad parked the car beside them. Mummy lifted brothers.
Topsy up to drop the bottles into the bottle bank.
SMASH went the first one as Topsy dropped it in.

"h dear!" said Tim. "They won't be able to use that ttle again."

"It doesn't matter," said Dad. "All the glass will be melted down and made into nice new bottles."

PAPER

The plastic bottles had to be squashed flat before they went into their bank. Topsy and Tim were champion bottle squas█████ "My fleece jacket is made from recycled plastic bottles," said Mummy. Topsy was amazed!

Tim helped Dad post the old newspapers into the paper bin.
"Newspaper is made from chopped down trees," said Dad.
"Recycling saves lots of trees."
"Great!" said Tim.

"Now we will do our shopping," said Mummy. "We will read all the labels and choose the things that do the world the least harm."

ummy chose free-range eggs for Topsy and
Tim's breakfast.

"These were laid by happy hens," said Mummy.

Dad chose organic carrots.
"No nasty chemicals on these," he said.
"I love carrots," said Tim.

"These toilet rolls are made from recycled paper,"
said Mummy. "That will save some trees."
"Good!" said Topsy.

On the way home they stopped at a garage for petrol.
"Miss Terry says cars are very bad," said Tim. "They make the air all smelly and yucky."

"Perhaps we should stop using the car so much,"
said Mummy.
"I suppose I could bike to work," said Dad.

When they got home Topsy and Tim went to play in the garden.
"I wish we had a wild-life garden, like the one at school, with
wild flowers and ladybirds and bees," said Topsy.
"And a pond for frogs," said Tim.

Dad came out to cut the grass.

"Please Dad, could we have a corner of the garden, just for wild-life?" said Topsy.

"You wouldn't need to cut the grass in the wild-life corner," said Tim.

"A wild-life corner is a great idea," said Dad.

Mummy liked the idea of a wild-life garden, too. "You will need some water for the wild things to drink or swim in," she said. "Your old sand-pit would make a good pond."

Mummy helped to dig a hole in a sunny corner of the garden. They put the old sand-pit in the hole, then Topsy and Tim carried water to it in their seaside buckets.

Topsy planted a tuft of grass in a flower pot and stood it in the middle of their pond.

"That's a little island for dragonflies," she said.

Tim piled stones on the
bottom of the pond.
"That's a cave for frogs
to hide in," he said.

Kerry came to see Topsy and Tim's wild-life garden.
"I like your pond," she said.
"It used to be our sand-pit, but we recycled it,"
said Tim, proudly.

Tim and Dad are shopping for vegetables.
Dad chooses organic carrots.
Look at the five jigsaw pieces.
Can you work out where each piece will fit?

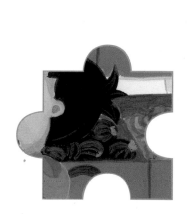

A Map of the Village

farm

Topsy and Tim's house

Tony's house

Kerry house

park

garage

post office

health centre

church

primary school

nursery school

police station

Illustrations by Belinda Worsley

A catalogue record for this book is available from the British Library

This title is based on the Topsy and Tim Green Activity Book
Published by Ladybird Books Ltd
A Penguin Company
Penguin Books Ltd., 80 Strand, London WC2R 0RL, UK
Penguin Books Australia Ltd., Camberwell, Victoria, Australia
Penguin Group (NZ) 67 Apollo Drive, Rosedale, North Shore 0632, New Zealand

1 3 5 7 9 10 8 6 4 2

ISBN: 978-1-40930-059-5
Printed in Italy